Little Fox's Best Friend

STORY BY MARCIA LEONARD • PICTURES BY KAREN SCHMIDT

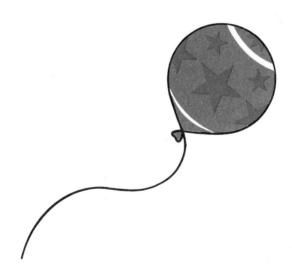

A Packard/Montgomery Book

BANTAM BOOKS
TORONTO • NEW YORK • LONDON • SYDNEY • AUCKLAND

For Michael and Zena. — *ML*

For Norman and Marie. — *KS*

RL 1, 003-006

LITTLE FOX'S BEST FRIEND
A Bantam Book / May 1987
First published in the United Kingdom by Transworld Publishers Ltd.

CHOOSE YOUR OWN ADVENTURE ® *is a registered trademark of*
Bantam Books, Inc.
Registered in U.S. Patent and Trademark Office and elsewhere.
Original conception of Edward Packard.
YOUR FIRST ADVENTURE is a trademark of Bantam Books, Inc.
Produced by Cloverdale Press Inc.

Bantam Books are published by Bantam Books, Inc. Its trademark, consisting of the
words "Bantam Books" and the portrayal of a rooster, is registered in U.S. Patent
and Trademark Office and in other countries. Marca Registrada. Bantam Books,
Inc., 666 Fifth Avenue, New York, New York 10103.

PRINTED IN THE UNITED STATES OF AMERICA

0 9 8 7 6 5 4 3 2 1

YOUR FIRST ADVENTURE™

A CONCEPT TO GROW WITH

How to use this book:

Your First Adventure books are perfect for reading aloud to young children. Just start with page two—this will set the scene and create a "let's pretend" mood. Go on to page four and let the child choose which of the two story paths to follow. Then continue reading until you reach the very happy ending.

Your First Adventure books are special in several ways: They allow children to participate actively in the story by presenting them with a choice. They provide young readers with two complete stories in each book. And they encourage children to identify with the realistic yet appealing experiences of the animal characters. All together the Your First Adventure series adds up to a library of colorful storybooks that children will enjoy at every reading.

Pretend you are a little fox and your best friend
is a little lamb who lives right next door.
Today is her birthday, and you are invited to her party.
But the two of you have had a fight, and now you're not
sure if you want to go to the party after all.

"You don't *have* to go," says your mom. "But if you stay at home, you'll have to play on your own. I have a lot of work to do today."

If you stay at home, you could play with your new toy castle. But maybe you'd rather go to the party— even though you're still mad at your friend.

If you decide to stay home and play, go on to page 5.
If you decide to go to the party, turn to page 11.

You go upstairs to your room and play with your castle.
You have a pretty good time—until you hear noises
coming from next door.

It's the kids at the birthday party! They're having
a sack race, and everyone is laughing and cheering.
It looks like fun.

6

"I don't care," you say. "I'm having fun, too."
And you sit down at your table and draw.
But a little later, some balloons float by.

7

Now the kids are playing Pin the Tail on the Donkey, and they all have party favors and balloons!

8

You're missing out on a great party. What's more, you miss
your best friend! "I guess I'll read for a while," you say.
But then a delicious smell floats through the window.

9

The kids are getting ready to have lunch. You see
the hot dogs on the grill—and then suddenly
your friend sees you! "Come on down!" she calls.
So you rush right over to her backyard.

Turn to page 17.

You go to the party, but you and your friend avoid
each other. You feel shy and embarrassed. And
when her mom lines everyone up for a sack race,
you try to hide.

She sees you anyway and gives you a sack. Then the
race is on—and it's really a lot of fun!

You feel a little better now. But you still haven't talked to
your friend. Maybe *this* will get her attention.

13

It works!
Your friend laughs, and so does everyone else.

Next you play Blind Man's Bluff. When your friend
is "it," they spin her around and around.

15

Then everybody else runs away. But you stand very still,
so that the one she catches is you!

16

"I'm sorry we had a fight," you say.
"I'm sorry, too," says your friend. "But I'm glad
that you're here. Without you, I wouldn't
have a happy birthday."

17

When lunch is ready, you get to sit next to your friend at the birthday table.

And when it's time to cut the cake, she makes sure that you get a piece with extra frosting.

19

You have a wonderful time at the rest of the party,
playing games and singing songs with all the kids. But
best of all, you and your friend are *best* friends again!

CHOOSE YOUR OWN ADVENTURE®

BOOKS TO GROW WITH

Dear Reader:

    If you liked my story, you will want to meet all of my friends in the other Your First Adventure books.

    When you get bigger, you will also love to read these Skylark Choose Your Own Adventure books for readers ages seven to nine:

#1 THE CIRCUS	#21 MONA IS MISSING
#2 THE HAUNTED HOUSE	#22 THE EVIL WIZARD
#3 SUNKEN TREASURE	#23 THE POLAR BEAR EXPRESS
#4 YOUR VERY OWN ROBOT	#24 THE MUMMY'S TOMB
#5 GORGA, THE SPACE MONSTER	#25 THE FLYING CARPET
#6 THE GREEN SLIME	#26 THE MAGIC PATH
#7 HELP! YOU'RE SHRINKING	#27 ICE CAVE
#8 INDIAN TRAIL	#28 FIRE!
#9 DREAM TRIPS	#29 THE FAIRY KIDNAP
#10 THE GENIE IN THE BOTTLE	#30 RUNAWAY SPACESHIP
#11 THE BIGFOOT MYSTERY	#31 LOST DOG!
#12 THE CREATURE FROM MILLER'S POND	#32 BLIZZARD AT BLACK SWAN INN
#13 JUNGLE SAFARI	#33 HAUNTED HARBOR
#14 THE SEARCH FOR CHAMP	#34 ATTACK OF THE MONSTER PLANTS
#15 THE THREE WISHES	#35 THE MISS LIBERTY CAPER
#16 DRAGONS!	#36 THE OWL TREE
#17 WILD HORSE COUNTRY	#37 HAUNTED HALLOWEEN PARTY
#18 SUMMER CAMP	#38 SAND CASTLE
#19 TOWER OF LONDON	#39 CARAVAN
#20 TROUBLE IN SPACE	#40 THE GREAT EASTER BUNNY ADVENTURE

    And when you get even older, there are lots of pocket-sized Choose Your Own Adventure books for readers ages ten and up. These wonderful stories will take you back in time, up in space, inside a race car, through a creepy castle and to many other exciting places.

    Hundreds of adventures are waiting for you! I sure hope you enjoyed mine. Thank you very much.

Sincerely,

Little Fox